# Rylee Fir
# Family
### a happy puppy tale

## by Jillian Lee

*Follow your dreams, work hard & keep reading!* ♡♡

*Jillian Lee*
*With love from Rylee*

ADOPT
-A-
PUPPY

tweet!
tweet!

Find Rylee's helper
Peachy, the lovebird,
in every scene!

For Pete, Ellie, Sydney, Piper, Rylee & Stormy

Rylee began a journey,
on a warm and sunny day.
She bounded up the stairs,
so happy she'd found her way!

"This is my new home," she thought.
"This is where I'll belong.
Where is my new family?
I've been waiting for sooo long!"

Rylee was so excited,
her tail wiggled even more!
"How many puppies will I find?
One or two? Three?! Or maybe four!"

"Time to find out," she smiled,
hopping up from the doormat...

...but inside, Rylee quickly froze...

...barking "WHAT IS THAT?!"

Rylee looked around
from where she now sat,
barking louder this time...

Finally now a little scared,
(from the lizard thing and the gray cat)
Rylee broke into her loudest howl…

"…AND WHAT, OH WHAT IS THAT?!"

"But *those things* are not puppies!"
Rylee worried while covering one eye.
"Will they be nice? Will they share?"
"I'll be brave," she woofed, "or at least I'll try!"

But the big room was empty now.
They were all missing, OH NO!
Rylee trotted around sniffing,
"Where, oh where did EVERYONE GO?!"

sniff!
sniff!

Rylee looked under the bed,
there was no one to be found.

So she checked in the garden, but there was only one sound.

ribbit!

ribbit!

ribbit!

ribbit!

ribbit!

She went digging and searching
through all the fresh clean clothes,
but still Rylee found **NOTHING!**

Just funny socks with *little* toes.

Rylee explored up high...

...and she scouted down low.
But still she had no clues,
as to where they would go.

A brave Rylee even looked
where it was too dark to see...

...*still nothing.* "JUST WHERE, OH WHERE, COULD THEY ALL POSSIBLY BE?!?!"

Disappointed and lonely,
Rylee settled down for a nap.
She was fast asleep *when...*

...suddenly, she felt a soft **tap!**

Rylee then opened one eye,
so she could finally see...

...all the different members
of her brand new family!

She snuggled in close to them
(and her very own bone!)
This really was the nicest,
most wonderful loving home.

Now Rylee could dream,
they had shown her the key...

...to being just as happy
as any puppy could be.

The end.

Made in the USA
Middletown, DE
29 April 2023

29575967R00015